Title and Subtitle

Title: The Joined Mates

Subtitle: Werewolf Shifter MF Romance Story

From the Author:

Thank you for purchasing this book.

Table of Contents

Title and Subtitle 1

Copyright 2

The Joined Mates 4

Description 4

Chapter 1 5

Chapter 2 10

Chapter 3 19

Chapter 4 28

The Joined Mates
Description

James Wolfe sat in the cafeteria of Copper Hills High School lost within the vision that sat 43 feet away from him. He knew it was exactly 43 feet because she sat at the same table, the same seat, at exactly the same time of day...that and he had measured out the approximate distance with his cousin Marcus two weeks after beginning their sophomore year. She was predictable and fastidious to the point of anal retention. This only strengthened his longing for her...his future mate. This presented two distinct problems...well three if you consider her track record with trouble and the statistical inevitability that she would be waist deep in it until they were properly mated.

The first problem was she didn't know she was his mate, that they were destined with the blessing of the Fates and Mother Luna to spend the rest of eternity together and bear many, many children. The thought alone of her round belly filled with his pups and full round breasts laden with sweet milk was enough to make him instantly hard and his inner wolf howl with need and want.

He was prepared to do anything to see that he and Rachel were properly mated. Even if she would not acknowledge his existence, he would protect her to his dying breath until it was time to properly reveal himself. But James had always been proactive in his pursuits and he was always one to think outside the box. If he could not be with Rachel in a romantic or social sense until after the Rites of Ascension, he would be with her in spirit. He would be her protector and guardian angel...scratch that...he would be her guardian wolf.

Chapter 1

James was at his usual spot during lunch period staring longingly at the woman of his desires and his dreams. He was thinking how lovely she looked with her long brown hair draping down her lithe body in ringlets. She was short. She was only 5' 2" but she was not really petite. She was curvy and voluptuous in all the right ways. At a 115 pounds, she had some curves but they were all in the right places. From her mouthwatering heart-shaped ass to her large breasts, James knew with a quiet certainty that her assets would only appreciate with age. God, you have to love how that interest accumulates.

James' mood certainly took a turn for the worst as he spied Rachel's current "boyfriend" approach. Jayden Michaels was the typical Neanderthal football player with the personality and charisma of a lump of moldy cheese and an IQ to match. This kid was so dense and oblivious to things outside his immediate interest, James wondered if with a bit more persuasion this guy may actually collapse into his own black hole.

"Jayden, I said stop!" James heard Rachel scream at the top of her lungs forcing everyone in the lunch room to immediately toward the disturbance.

"Damn babe! Watch it with the pipes. I was just trying to get a little loving from you. Can you blame a guy for trying to get a little something from his girl?" Jayden pleaded shamelessly.

"You are such a fucking Neanderthal. I am not your 'girl'. I will not be one of your bimbo bitches that drop to their knees the minute you ask them. You are a fucking pig and I don't want to see you again. You fucking disgust me!"

Rachel eyes were clouded with a fury that was unnatural...well...supernatural.

James followed Rachel's movements with his eyes as she quickly made her way out of the cafeteria and waited to see if Jayden would be stupid enough to follow. God, he hoped this fucker was that stupid. His wolf was practically pleading with him to cripple this fucker for life and remove the option for procreation. But Jayden simply yelled an indiscernible obscenity in her general direction and return to grazing like the common bovine he was.

Rachel stumbled blindly toward her locker. Her eyes streaming tears clouding her vision as she fought with the tumbler, getting the combination wrong three times before she cursed silently and forced herself to calm down. Why did she always allow herself to be drawn to the Alpha losers in school? Why couldn't she find someone who loved her for her mind and personality, not just because she was a cheerleader? Finally, after a couple minutes and some breathing exercises to reign in her erratic heartbeat she was able to open the locker. She was shocked to find sitting in her locker a polished ebony box. Her temper quickly rose to the top as she tried to determine who the fuck had violated her own private piece of public-school property. If that fucker Jayden was trying to buy her allegiance with some fucking trinkets, he had another fucking thing coming. Such an asshole!

But inside her head something assured her that this was not from the asshole but someone who would become eternally more important to her. A voice quietly whispered this was a start to something wonderful. Opening the box she was shocked to see a golden emblem embossed under the lid...a werewolf baying at the moon on a red shield in the center of a full moon...an exact match to the tattoo now gracing her lower body since she could remember...this was important! Inside the box was lined with dark emerald velvet and there were three items within: a small figurine of a wolf that she soon recognized was made out of jade...expensive. The second was a small red velvet jewelry box. She opened it to find a small golden pin that resembled angel wings....beautiful. The third was a small note on some very nice stationary.

To My Rachel ,

For the next time you think you can fly. A little reminder that I will always be there to catch you whenever you fall. With all my love and affection.

Your Guardian Wolf -- J.W.

Rachel read and reread the note again and again. Her guardian wolf...a personal protector...a sentinel to guide her in the darkness. She felt a warm feeling wash over her body like being wrapped in a down comforter. She felt a heat build in her lower abdomen and spread down between her legs. She felt her temperature rise and her breath come short as a burning sensation and a warm glow emanated below her. She thought of the man with emerald eyes who caught her in his arms last Friday... a man with gorgeous long hair that fell over his eyes, wild and untamed, her guardian wolf...a man who captured her heart in the instant that he caught her body and their eyes met for the first time.

She thought back to last weekend and the brief, precious seconds that altered her being forever. She remembered the sheer thrill and electricity that went through her body. She remembered how her body had molded instantly to his slight frame but felt as his iron hard muscles rippled beneath her...his body reminded her of a swimmer's...lean but powerful. Rachel remembered how her pussy had flooded and her temperature spiked as feelings of intense arousal had engulfed her heart and her mind like a forest fire. And as quickly as she felt his presence, he was gone with an apology spoken so softly it barely registered. She didn't even know who he was. She promised herself that soon...soon she would discover the identity to her guardian wolf.

James and Marcus were at their usual spot in the lunchroom arguing the merits and faults of the newest chips released by both Intel and AMD. Marcus was a diehard Intel fan and refused to acknowledge that AMD was anything other than a second-rate copycat that simply rode the Intel's corporate coat-tails and scooped up their sloppy seconds. James was furious. Not about Intel or AMD...he couldn't care less about that. He was mad at himself at how chicken-shit he was around Rachel. For the last three weeks he had tried working up his courage just to talk with her. The Rites of Ascension were here and he hadn't muttered a single syllable to her since the homecoming football game and his haphazard heroics on the field. He was supposed to meet her at his house tonight for the first arranged meeting and he hadn't brought himself to say "hello" to her yet. *This was fucking awesome! And he is supposed to be a fucking Alpha...real fucking great...a pussy Alpha in wolf form...God Damn It!*

What the fuck was he supposed to tell her?

"Hi there! Hey listen...I know we only met for like twenty seconds last week...but you're my intended and I wanted to invite you over to my house for a ceremony that will help explain what we are and why we are meant to be together as eternal mates for all of fucking eternity. And not

to mention I'm a werewolf and tonight I will reach my final form tonight so I won't simply look like a nerd pussy bitch anymore...I'll just act like one. Great! See you tonight! Love ya!"

This was going to be a fucking disaster.

"You just can't bring yourself to admit the newest Athlon X2 processors are just as powerful as Intel's Core 2. You are a stubborn, thickheaded Cro-Magnon that should be lumped with all the other football playing Homo Erectus," said James.

"That's a low fuckin' blow douche bag and you know it. I was simply stating with a larger L2 cache and higher benchmarks, the newest Core 2's are better suited dollar for dollar for the higher end PC's. And you can just go and lick your own ass for all I care wolf-boy," Marcus stated heatedly.

They were starting to gather stares. Including the surprised eyes of the one person James prayed would simply overlook him for now...shit...it was too soon.... wasn't it? Rachel was staring directly at him now and he felt the heated conflict build between his human and his wolf side. His human side wanted to dig a hole beneath the laminated surface of the cafeteria and die a slow and agonizing death from all the humiliation, and his wolf side was howling with joy that she finally recognized him and there was a spark of interest and... something else hidden in those jade pools of loveliness. His neck and ears had become crimson with all the blood flooding his veins and his heartbeat had increased to deafening as his embarrassment increased exponentially. James did the only thing his teenage mind could manage on such a level...flee. He bolted from the lunch room and headed for the nearest lavatory emptying the contents of his recently ingested lunch.

Chapter 2

Before Marcus could stop him, James had fled in an embarrassment induced panic, running down the nearest hall and crashing head long through the men's bathroom.

"James wait! Shit!" barked Marcus before chasing after his cousin in a dead run.

"James! James! You have to come out of the fucking bathroom man...you can't stay in there any longer. You've got shit to do...remember? You need to talk to her. You can't get around it any longer. I can't be the one to do this man. You are the only one she will listen to. You have put this off long enough dingus...pull off your pussy and grow a fucking pair! You are the fucking Alpha...start fucking acting like one! " James practically screamed this while banging loudly on the wooden door.

James sat barricaded against the door as he listened to his cousin rant and hammer against the wooden door. If Marcus wasn't careful, he could easily splinter the wood and then where would they be? But at the mention of the word "Alpha" a switch was thrown in James' head. His cousin was right. He couldn't puss out anymore. He had been acting like a lowly bitch ever since he had entered high school. He had let his weak human emotions and frailties govern his reactions to situations. He was an Alpha, bread to lead one of the most powerful clans in the supernatural world. He had let his weak nerdy persona, this shell he had carefully manufactured to protect himself and his mate, override his core personality. He was wolf at heart. He was ALPHA. He felt his wolf howl and leap in triumph as he finally recognized and embraced his true destiny. He had grown into his own...he had grown a set...he had discovered his natural, baser nature and found the courage hidden within.

He was ready to claim his mate. He was ready to claim his birth right.

James leapt to his feet feeling a weight that had hung over his shoulders and dampened his spirits and his heart for too long fall away leaving behind a sense of purpose—a sense of pride—a sense of devotion and longing to finally be himself and show Rachel the true man he could be. The man she loved and deserved. He opened the bathroom door with such force he nearly dislocated Marcus's shoulder as he continued to pound on the door and jiggle the handle (pun intended). Marcus looked at him with suspicion and concern until he saw the determined look that now governed James' countenance, a look that only a man that had finally embraced his true self could show. The look was of an Alpha.

"About fucking time! I was starting to seriously doubt the Fates. I thought they had finally succumbed to senility. Go get her bro. She's waiting for you," Marcus said with a grin as he cleared a path to let James's past.

James walked with purpose and direction as he confidently strolled over to Rachel Merchant. He caught her looking at him with a mixture of amazement and...sniff...yep lust. This may be easier than he originally thought. With a sudden surge of bravado and confidence, James walked over to her and wrapping his arms around her small frame he lifted her up and planted a gentle yet firm kiss on Rachel's lips. This kiss was meant to convey all of his pent up emotions and desires. The resulting effects sent fireworks shooting off behind both of their eye sockets and making them moan in mutual appreciation. The kiss deepened until they were battling each other's tongues in a duel to see who could search out the other's mouth the fastest. When they finally broke James looked into Rachel's eyes to see a new found seed of love and devotion starting to germinate. He knew he had her at last.

Everyone left present in the lunchroom were too shocked at what was now displayed before their very eyes to utter a response. Something like this was unheard of. A geek did not simply walk up to one of the hottest girls in the history of this school and plant a scorching kiss right on her lips. It just was not done. But James did not give a flying fuck for such juvenile high school social rules. This was his beloved he was about to claim. He would no longer allow himself to be swayed by such trivial matters again. He was an Alpha apparent, next in line to lead the Wolfe clan. He was going to start acting like it, God damn it!

"Rachel," he whispered so only she could hear, "my name is James Wolfe. I have something of endless importance that will affect us for the rest of our lives. Will you accompany me on a walk please? I promise you'll be completely safe with me. I would never allow anything to ever happen to you. I love you and care for you too deeply to allow that."

That last statement had apparently hit a chord deep within Rachel's heart. She was simply too stunned and suddenly out of breath to whisper a reply. She simply nodded her assent and took the hand offered her. Rachel knew the time had come. She didn't know what it was, but it was time for her to get some answers. The moment he took her hand she felt the warmth wash over her and she felt an eternal calmness envelop her. She felt safe and complete next to him. She melted into his side and let him lead them out the side doors toward the football field and the visitor uprights. This conversation would take place in the woods—his woods.

It was the most natural place for them, even if she didn't know it yet.

As they walked toward the forest clearing James could feel a pair of eyes burning a hole into the back of his head. He looked back toward the field and noticed one of the larger football linemen staring death back at him. Jayden Michaels was looking at the coupling with a mixture of anger and confusion. His eyes were darkening with a new feeling of jealous rage. Jayden had not witnessed the act in the lunch room but he had heard of it at the speed only capable under the physics of high school gossip. James could not help himself and he simply smiled and laughed at the darkening confusion and rage that were clearly clouding the poor idiot's face. He knew what was coming. He could smell the acidic tang of anger and rage building in Jayden. He knew he would have to deal with Jayden directly before they could have their conversation. And this conversation was too important to interrupt. He sighed heavily and turned as he saw the large brute lumbering toward them at an alarming speed.

She had chosen a nerd over him? The thought was incomprehensible. His feeble mind could not register how a beautiful girl such as she would choose someone like him. Something was wrong. And by damn he was going to find out and beat the shit out of the little nerd in the process. His primal brain screamed in rage as he broke formation and charged toward the rail thin nerd; his ears were deaf to the screams from his coaches. This was going to be too fucking sweet. He was going lay out this little cocksucker and enjoying rearranging that smug look on his face. Then he was going to take what was his from that little whore slut of a cock tease. He would not be denied what he felt was always his.

Too bad it seemed. People like Jayden would always learn the hard way and you had to beat it into their thick skulls before they learned. Some things are not for sale. Some things are not for consideration. Some things are not taken but earned . Some things are always off limits to everyone but a single person. And by the Fates Jayden was definitely not that person. James hated to tip his hand and show Rachel some of his power so early—he didn't want to scare her—but this lumbering piss ant was just praying for it. Besides his wolf had not had any exercise in some time and he was anxious for a work out. If Jayden had to be the poor bastard to give his wolf an outlet for his frustration, so be it.

Jayden zeroed in on the little fucker now staring at him with a mixture of mild amusement and boredom. The fool actually looked at him like he pitied Jayden. The fucking cocksucker didn't know what was going to hit him. When he was within six feet of James he lunged at the nerd with the force of 240 pounds of rippling muscle.

With maniacal rage Jayden roared, "You're fucking dead nerd!"

But something was off. He was mere inches from wrapping his fingers around the scrawny nerd's neck when the little prick disappeared. He suddenly felt an excruciating pain seize his back as James brought down a karate chop directed at the center of his spine. Jayden dropped like a sack of potatoes as he crumpled into the ground. His excessive momentum carried his body along the ground another two feet before coming to rest. As Jayden forced himself to a standing position, a large piece of sod was lodged into his face mask temporarily blinding him. He ripped off the helmet with a primal roar trying to locate the source of all his hatred and aggression. James stood directly in front of him waiting.

James continued to look at Jayden with that mixture of resignation and pity as if to say, "do we really have to do this?" Jayden simply got an evil grin as he reached into the waistband of his pants to recover the brass knuckles hidden beneath. He loved these things. They always added a little something extra to his already aggressive nature. Slipping the new weapon over his hand he prepared for a new assault upon the little asshole. Before he could take a new stance, a small ball of fury was on his back, clawing and scratching at his face and pulling his hair out by the roots. Jayden rolled his wait forward launching Rachel to the ground.

"You fucking little whore! You cheating little slut! How dare you choose him over me!" Jayden screamed hysterically.

Before Rachel could rise to a crouching position to ready for another attack, she dropped the large clump of hair that she had managed to retrieve from Jayden's scalp. Jayden looked down at the parcel that now lay on the ground. He reached to the back of his head to discover a large bald spot above his neck line.

"You fucking bitch! You're going to pay for that. After I send that little cocksucker over there into a coma, you and I have unfinished business to attend to. I am going to get what rightfully is mine. I will not be denied. You are going to give me everything I have coming to me," Jayden said this with a wicked, maniacal gleam in his eye.

Rachel did not offer a reply but simply launched herself into his body, aiming for his eyes hoping to do some major damage before James got hurt. Jayden caught her in midair by the throat and with a backhand with the brass knuckles he smashed her to the ground. Her lower lip and chin were bleeding. She was having trouble keeping conscious.

Before Jayden could revel in the sight of this slut bleeding and cowering beneath him, Jayden felt his right shoulder wrenched out of its socket as his hand was pulled back and up toward his spine. A foot came out, crushing the back of his knee cap. The force of the blow was so great Jayden could feel his patella snap. Jayden fell to his knees in an instant. He groaned in excruciating pain. Son of a bitch! He had completely forgotten about the nerd. Where the hell did this little dipshit get so much power?

James was livid. He was having the hardest time not transforming in front of the entire football team and ripping this bastard's head and spinal column from his body. His wolf was howling with pure rage. Someone had dared to lay a hand on their mate. Retribution and blood were demanded. James had to usher up every last ounce of his willpower to quiet the blood lust now coursing through his veins as his wolf clawed at him, trying to gain dominance over his body.

James looked down at Jayden with a righteous fury. This pathetic excuse for congealed matter had dared to lay a hand on his Rachel. With a sudden malicious delight, James strengthened his grip on the offending hand crushing every major bone in Jayden's hand. He would need several weeks of surgery, reconstruction, and physical therapy before he even hoped to use it again. Jayden howled with a pain so great tears were streaming out of the linebacker's...ahem....FORMER linebacker's eyes. James suddenly felt a warm liquid dripping on his shoes. The cowardly bastard had pissed himself. James smiled wickedly.

He lowered his head to Jayden's right ear and whispered so neither Rachel nor anyone else could hear.

"I am only going to say this once you cock sucking mother fucker! If I ever see, hear, or smell you within 50 feet of Rachel again I swear to all the dark Gods that I will sever your spinal column from your head, tear out your jugular, and shit down your throat. Rachel is my mate...my life. No one ever lays a hand on her. No one! "James tightened his grip on the fractured hand forcing Jayden to whimper, "No one raises a hand in violence to her, especially a worthless sack of shit like you. I will kill you if I ever see you near her again. And don't expect to play again this year...or any year...and I fully intend on pressing charges for your unprovoked and ill conceived aggression."

And with a dark growl that seemed to emanate from deep within James that had Jayden whimpering in utter terror, James lifted Jayden and threw him by the already dislocated shoulder, ripping the bastard's rotator cuff completely, into the visiting uprights. Luckily, James was merciful enough to aim for the well padded side beams and not the bare steel of the cross bar. Jayden hit face first, breaking his nose in the padded beam and crumpled into unconsciousness.

James yelled to the head coach to get an ambulance and to call the cops. He went over to where Rachel sat stunned and disoriented and kneeled down before her. He gingerly placed a hand on her head. She started to shy away but with a pained look from James her fear was forgotten in an instance and she allowed him to run his fingers through her silky tresses causing her body to shudder and a warm puddle of arousal to pool in her panties. James gently lifted

Rachel up as if she were weightless and settled her on her feet.

"We have to get that cut looked at and have a short chat with the officers. Then I fully intend on finishing our walk. We still have much to discuss before tonight," James said.

Rachel started to question what was going to happen tonight but smartly decided to let the issue lie at the moment. She saw James in a whole new light. She had watched with utter disbelief as James moved with inhuman strength and speed to stop and disarm her would-be attacker. If she had not witnessed the whole thing with her own eyes, she would never have believed a word of it. James was beyond human. He was strong, swift, and gorgeous—.a triple threat. And when she heard that animalistic growl that seemed to reverberate through his entire body, it sent shivers of lust shooting through every synapse in her tiny body. She wanted this man...and he was definitely a man. She didn't know why, but she was falling fast for her guardian wolf.

Chapter 3

The police and ambulance arrived a few minutes later after the head coach had phoned 911 to report the fight. The EMT's looked at the carnage that was Jayden Michael's in utter disbelief. This kid was a solid 225-240 of solid muscle. The other guy was barely a buck fifty. Jayden had a broken nose, three bruised and two broken ribs, dislocated right shoulder, torn rotator cuff (probably with every tendon severed along with it), a fractured patella (probably a blown ACL as well), and a right hand that looked to be completely crush. The paramedics looked at James with a look of utter shock and respect. If the kid could do this, James was a bad-ass mother fucker. You did not want to fuck with this kid.

Of course, Rachel was not to be dismissed. The little hellion had done some damage. Along with a large tuft of hair that was now sitting in evidence baggies, Jayden had four-inch claw marks down both of his cheeks, and a large scratch down the front of his throat where Rachel clung to when Jayden threw her.

The cops had already taken James and Rachel's statements and were now questioning a field of students and faculty. The football team had been excused to the locker rooms after a cursory set of questions. The head and assistant coaches who were closest to the action were helpful in clearing James of any wrong doing. They clearly explained what unfolded and included careful insight into Jayden's anger issues and control problems. The brass knuckles found on Jayden's still mangled right hand was the last nail in his coffin. The kid was looking at some serious charges including assault with a deadly weapon. But with Jayden's extensive injuries and a long road to recovery that would probably extend to a year or more, the cops were hesitant to make an arrest.

James was the one who came up with the solution. His father was close friends with several judges and with a small battalion of corporate lawyer's backing up his son, there was little question to the future of Jayden if James decided to press full charges. But without adding too much insult to extensive injury James decided to be the bigger man and hopefully get a young man turned around before his life was completely in the shitter.

He said he would not press charges if Jayden, after sufficient convalescence, was immediately expelled, forced into anger management and extensive counseling, and had a restraining order placed on him that forbade him from contact of any kind with James or Rachel within 500 feet...phone calls and electronic correspondence included. The cops were quick to agree and promised to quickly draw up the necessary documentation with the lawyers and have a judge sign it before end of the night.

When Christopher Michaels was called, he was obviously upset at the injuries Jayden sustained but was more than aware of his son's emotional and anger issues. His son had been angry since his mother had died several years earlier, never really coming to grips with the loss. His son had closed himself off to any form of fatherly or professional support and quickly found an outlet in bullying and being just a general asshole as his only way to vent his sense of loss and abandonment. When James called his father to explain the situation, Robert was quick to offer Christopher a deal that would help both parties...and maybe get Jayden on the right track to a better future. Robert agreed to pay all medical costs including counseling for Jayden in return that he completes all court required counseling and anger management classes and with a sworn promise that he would abide by the rules of the restraining order. Mr. Michaels was ecstatic and quickly agreed to everything. Chris was a long and faithful employee at one of Mr. Wolfe's companies and was never amazed more at the generosity and kindness of an employer than Robert Wolfe. The whole situation was settled within an hour of the fight and James and Rachel were free to have that little chat.

James and Rachel walked slowly into the forest holding hands. They had quickly made and exit after everything was settled with the police and after the EMT's had cleaned and dressed Rachel's wound. It was nothing serious, just a split lip that would be tender for a few days and a few scratches and bruised chin. James guided them to a clearing between the Douglas Fir that he knew so well. He often came here with his brother's when they wanted to run and work off some aggression toward each other. There was a set of set of stone markers noting the cardinal and secondary compass points. A wooden bench was carved into a very large oak that seemed out of place among the pine. It was the oldest living tree in the forest and was planted when the Wolfe Clan first moved to this area.

"What is this place James? It's absolutely gorgeous," Rachel asked clearly struck by the simple beauty.

"It's a place that I come to think or work off some aggression with my brothers. Whenever we have had enough sparring or workouts at the family gym, we come here to let ourselves run wild and free," James said.

"Rachel...what do you know of your surname Merchant?"

"Not much...my parents tell me it's a very old and proud name but the're kind of cryptic when I pry a little more. They keep saying that I'll find out very soon enough, but they can't tell me more."

"They really couldn't. It is part of the binding agreement set down by the Articles of Council set at Nicaea," James whispered.

Rachel understood none of this....council of what?

"Rachel. Do you believe in soul mates? Two people destined for one another from birth. Set on this Earth for each other and no one else?" he asked.

Rachel slowly nodded her head. She did indeed believe in soul mates but was unsure where this was headed even though her heart was screaming the painfully obvious at her.

James reached out and quietly lifted her shirt up just enough to bare her belly button then proceeded to slowly unzip Rachel's pants. Rachel tried to raise a voice of objection but was only able to amount to a small squeak. James undid the button of her denim jeans then lowered them until they sagged on her knees. He then, ever so gently lowered her panties until it revealed her tattoo.

"How...how did you know about my tattoo? I have had this thing forever...as long as I can remember...even as a little girl. Every time I try and ask my parents about it, they simply tell me it is a mark of extreme importance and I will find out on my 18th birthday. They have never elaborated beyond that."

James quickly lifted his black t-shirt. His pale skin glistened in the early afternoon sun that parted the thick canopy of trees. He turned his left bicep so Rachel could clearly see the matching tattoo stamped on his skin. Rachel lost all control of her respiratory system and began to hyperventilate. James had to lower her down to the bench and comfort her for a few minutes before he got her breathing back to normal. After a few minutes Rachel's breathing was back to normal but James could clearly hear her heartbeat moving at a fast pace.

"Rachel. I was born at St. Luke's Memorial hospital on October 3rd, 1988 at 2:21 am in room 102. A little girl was born two minutes later in the bed next to my mother. This little girl was the daughter of Brian and Natalie Merchant, employees and close friends to my father and mother, Robert and Margaret Wolfe. That early morning a full moon bathed both babies in its light...the light of Mother Luna. The three Fates have decreed that we are meant for each other...kindred souls bound to each other for all eternity. They placed these sacred tattoos upon our bodies to signify our binding and to help us identify each other. See?"

James moved closer to Rachel as she sat relaxed in the hollow of the tree. James caressed her gently then wrapped her body in his arms. Rachel felt a warm tingle where her tattoo lay and looked down. Her tattoo was glowing! How? She looked at James and seeing the confusion in her eyes he gently moved her head to look at his bicep now draped over her left shoulder. His tattoo was also glowing brightly. The blue moon shined brightly on his arm and the wolf on the crest seemed to move of his own volition.

"We are mates my dearest Rachel. We have destined to be together forever, to love each other, to marry and have children. I know it seems confusing, far-fetched, even crazy, but it is the truth. I promise you now here in this holy place. I have never and will never lie to you...ever. I can't. It isn't in my nature to be deceitful but a mate can't lie to the other; it is physically impossible. Sometimes I must withhold something from you for security reasons or to protect you and the pack, but I promise on my life and sacred honor that I will never lie to you," James said this with his heart and soul lay bare to her scrutiny. He didn't know what would happen if she rejected him here. It would destroy him.

"James. I'm confused. I get why I have the tattoo but I don't get what it means. I mean I don't understand the wolf and crest. Why is the wolf look like something out of a horror movie? James, I"m falling hard, fast, and deep for you. And I can already tell you hold a deep love and respect for me. But I need to know more. Help me understand," Rachel said almost in a whisper.

James understood. He sighed heavily because he must show Rachel what he truly was; what she would soon become. He would never hide anything from her, never again.

"Rachel. I need you to trust me now. Trust me when I say I love you and would protect you and defend you to my dying breath. I would never raise a finger to you in anger or do something you would not approve of. I love you with all my heart and what I do next may be shocking, but it must be done before we can be together. Do you trust me sweetheart?" James pleaded.

Rachel looked at the man she had only met a few days ago but was undeniably attracted to and quickly coming to understand the depth of her feelings for him.

"Yes, James. I do trust you. I trust you with my life, my heart, my soul, and my love." She said these words with a conviction she did not know she had. She quickly reviewed her statement and discovered she meant every word.

James stood quietly and continued where his shirt left off. He quickly unbuttoned his pants and lowered them off his body with his socks and shoes. With a mischievous grin James hooked his fingers in his boxers while looking directly at Rachel. He noticed her breath catch in anticipation. He lowered his underwear to the forest floor and stood in his entire masculine, all be it pale, glory.

Rachel gasped with an audible squeak. James was not large. He was fucking huge. Her brain began to run rampant with all sorts of naughty and lascivious fantasies. Her breath began to quicken as she felt her core temperature sky rocket and her pussy begin to water the wooden seat beneath her. Would that thing ever fit in her? God! It looked like it would tear her in two. It must be at least 8 inches long and he wasn't even hard.

James looked at Rachel as a myriad of emotions ran over her face....awe, shock, disbelief, hunger, and lust. He could smell the deep cedar musk of her arousal; he was practically drowning in her scent it was so strong. His cock immediately began to stiffen and harden as his arousal came full circle. Before he knew it his cock had grown to its full length of twelve inches. It bounced with anticipation and began to drip copious amounts of precum all over the pine needles and moss. He wanted to do something with it immediately, but he had to focus his mind on more important matters. He began to feel his bones crack as they shifted and allowed the change to come over him. He had long gotten used to the mild discomfort that came with shifting. When it was all said and done there was a massive midnight black wolf with amber green eyes that stood four feet to the head staring back at Rachel's now ashen glare.

Rachel could not believe it. One moment she is creaming over James'cock, devising all sorts of schemes to get that massive staff of manhood shoved into her dripping cunt, and the next she is sitting before a gorgeous black wolf that was twice as large as the largest timber wolf she had ever known to be in existence. She wanted to scream, to run, but her body would not run, would not operate. Her body had fucking struck on her and management was out to lunch with no sign of returning. She looked incredulously at the massive beast now standing a few feet away from her waiting patiently for her to make the first move.

"James?"

The black wolf yipped and began to wag its tail like an overgrown puppy. The wolf lowered himself to his belly and crept forward in abject subjugation until his muzzle rested at her feet.

"James? Is that you?"

Yes. It's me!

"Who said that?"

I said that!

"Where are you?"

Right in front of you Rachel, I'm transmitting my thoughts to you.

"Seriously, who said that?"

I did! The voice said with an edge of impatience,

"Who?"

ME!!!

She looked at the wolf and with a giggle she winked at him to know she was only playing with him now.

Fuck! I should have seen that one coming.

"Now, now baby. Language sweetheart! What would the children say?"

They would say to take mommy to bed and fuck her into submission until she learns her place.

"Promises, promises big boy. You haven't tamed me yet."

The wolf now sat on his haunches and placed his muzzle to her panties. The annoying piece of fabric that had protected her maidenhood had become an obstacle to his desire. Before Rachel could even form the objection in her mind, James reached out with his teeth and tore he panties right off her hips.

"Hey! I liked that pair wolf-boy!"

I'll buy you all the panties you want. They were keeping me from my prize.

"Prize? What..."

Chapter 4

Before Rachel could finish James had moved closer and shoved his muzzle right into her sex. With his long, wolfish tongue he began to feast upon her womanly delights. She was heavenly! She tasted like...like...well fuck...he couldn't place the flavor at this particular time and place...his brain had taken a back seat to his taste buds and the necessary mechanics of his tongue to bring her pleasure.

"Oh SHIT! God fucking damn it! Don't....don't ...st..stop"

Rachel lost all the necessary functions to utter coherent speech. She simply allowed the feelings of intense heat and lust rush over her in waves.

Fucking sneaky bastard!

I heard that!

"What?" Rachel suddenly asked between gasps of pleasurable shudders.

I said I heard that. Baby we're mates! We can talk telepathically. I can hear you and you can hear me. Just let yourself go and enjoy the pleasure and you can swear at me in your head all you want...okay?

Whatever you want sneaky bas..bas...oh fuck that feels fantastic! Baby! James! Don't you ever fucking stop loving my fuck hole, you hear me? This is incredible. Oh God! James. Eat me...devour me...fucking take me...love me and never fucking stop!

With that James growled in triumph and doubled his efforts in bringing his love pleasure. He shoved his tongue deep into her tunnel until it bumped into her virginity. With a slight cringe Rachel jumped a bit and squeaked in pain.

Sorry baby! I'm trying to be gentle. I won't break it now. I want it to be in a proper bed and at a proper time.

Thank you, James! I love you!

I love you to baby!

James continued his assault upon her senses as he gently plunged his tongue into her sweltering fuck hole again and again. When his cold nose bumped into her clitoris Rachel lost it. She started grinding her sex hard against James mouth and mewling in pure heat. She was insatiable. She only wanted that sweet release, that little death that would relieve her of all this sweet torturous pressure that had been building in her.

Without notice Rachel went off with a bang. She squirted her cream all over James muzzle and tongue, startling him enough to back up a foot. Rachel continued to squirt heavy streams of cum ejaculating from her urethra. James quickly launched himself back in with relish to retrieve the sweet offering of her spending. This forced Rachel to scream again as her orgasm was prolonged as James continued to lap and nuzzle her sex until she couldn't stand it anymore, shoving him away quickly.

Holy fuck baby! That was amazing! I didn't know you squirted. Oh God. I'm going to have such fun bringing you off like that. That was unbelievable. I loved it!

I...I...holy fucking Gods in heaven, hell, wherever...I had no idea I could do that. James love. That was the best...best fucking orgasm I have ever had.

Better than the orgasms that little pocket rocket you bought last year brings you?

How do you know about that?!!

She could hear James chuckling in her head almost to the point of laughing hysterically. She looked at him quizzically to see the wolf smiling a wolfish grin and his tail wagging frantically. His eyes were full of mirth and mischief.

I have a confession baby. Your parents have been feeding me and my family information about you, your passions, your likes, dislikes...your...um...extracurricular activities for years now.

She could hear the wolf almost giggle.

It is part of the mating contract they entered into before we were born. They would supply my family information to help me learn about you and what makes you tick. Over the last two millennia mated families have learned to share close personal information with each other. It helps not only the potential mates, but it brings the mated families together, binding them one to the other. Don't be mad baby. They did it because they love you. They wanted me to be as prepared as possible when this time came. They love you and they love me. They know how crazy I am about you and they just want to see us happy.

"Traitorous, turn coat bastards," she huffed.

She was trying to be mad at them but the twinkle in her eyes and the corners of her mouth betrayed her false anger and she fell into bouts of giggling laughter.

"I am not mad, James! I know they only want what is best for me. And it looks and feels like that you are what is best." She beamed a wicked smile at him.

There was a brief moment of activity as James shifted back to his human form. A brief flash of fur and the crackling of bone and he was again as naked as the day he was born.

He sat quietly next to her not even bothering to put his pants back on. He simply held her tight and nuzzled her neck, licking and nibbling the side of her neck and up to her ear lobes. Rachel gasped as he gently probed her inner ear with his tongue.

"Like that?" he asked.

"Mmmmm," she purred, "I could definitely get used to this."

She stopped him after a couple of minutes before they both got carried away and decide to copulate right her on the forest floor.

"You never answered my original question. What is with the werewolf and shield? Seriously. We get off on some serious tangents with our conversation," she said this with a wicked lick and nip at his jaw which made him groan in lust.

Forcing his wolf and his manhood to settle back down, he forced his mind back to matters at hand. It wasn't dire information, but it would make the evening run much more smoothly. Besides, he didn't want to miss out on her birthday present and the night he had planned for them. Tonight would be their first night together if everything went right. He sighed and breathed for a moment to cool his jets then opened his eyes to look at those lovely jade pools of desire.

"God, you don't make this easy on me. I could get lost in your eyes for days on end..."

She snapped her fingers to bring back his attention.

"Focus here Romeo! Maybe you should put your pants on so I'M not distracted by that anaconda lying in your lap."

James had to laugh at her comment. The only thing he could think of the moment was a line from one of his favorite comedians.

Squirrel Man!

Huh? Squirrel? What are you going on about?
Nothing baby...I'll explain it later.

He chuckled and quickly moved to recover his jeans and t-shirt as she readjusted herself and righted her jeans back over her now battered and sore pussy. The coarse feeling of the denim sans panties against her lips was an unusual feeling, but not uncomfortable. It simply reminded her of why she was missing panties and the incredible ride James's oral skills had sent her on. She shook her head to clear the erotic fog that threatened to engulf her mind again. God what this man did to her!

"Okay now that all of the tasty bits of our desires are now safely camouflaged once more, we can continue our discourse of our oratory dissertation until completion."

God you are such a dork!

I know. But that makes you a dork by association.

She rolled her eyes at him, "get on with it!"

Yes, my lady.

"The wolf and shield is my family's crest...the Wolfe Clan. The werewolf is depicted in full battle form and the red background is for the blood and strength of our ancestors. You see over three thousand years ago there were five great people with many different clans...the elves, dwarves, humans, the vampires, and of course werewolves. The vampires and werewolves have been natural allies because of our affinity toward night and the moon. The humans, dwarves, and elves were also allies. Now you have to realize this is back when magic and superstition were still prevalent in the world. Humans still believed and lived among us supernatural creatures.

In 637 BC an elfin princess named Trinity from the Silver Leaf Coven was to wed a vampire prince named Dominion from the Crimson Fang brood. Just go with the names, they have changed over time. They don't mean what they used to. Anyway, the marriage was arranged by the fathers of both great houses and it was a political move. The families hoped to bridge the ever-growing rift between the two alliances that were held together by a shaky truce that was established in 723 BC. Before that time it was nothing but war and bloodshed between the different houses and factions. No one was getting along. So, they decided if they couldn't ensure a peace through treaties, they would breed one. The hope was for a child to be sired between vampire and elf to help bridge a genetic gap that had devastated blood lines for the past six centuries.

So, the wedding took place and Trinity was wed to Dominion. The marriage and the whole thing were doomed from the start. The two hated one another. They were furious at each other's parents and resented being used as pieces in a fucked up political game of chess. The two hated each other so much they stayed with their own people. They didn't even consummate their wedding night. The only reason the two finally sired a child is when Trinity came into heat. Dominion was literally dragged to the bed chamber by four of his brothers. Trinity was on the bed tied and gagged screaming her bloody head off. But once Dominion got a whiff of her arousal, his dick took over and he was on her like white on rice. There was no love between them. It was quick and dirty fucking. He mounted her, broke through her hymen, and twenty seconds later he ejaculated. She didn't even get a chance to have an orgasm. It is said she vomited each time after he came in her, she was that disgusted with her situation. This went on for three agonizing weeks until the healers determined that Trinity was finally pregnant. Dominion was gone the next day until the night Trinity went into labor. Again he was dragged kicking and screaming into the birthing room. It was an agonizing 18 hour ordeal. Finally the baby crowned and was delivered. But the baby was dead, it was a still birth. The labor had nearly killed Trinity. She was sick with a fever for two weeks and then went into isolation with her family until she again came into heat. The stupid bastards were just going to keep on trying. They were that desperate for a hybrid heir.

Trinity had other plans though. She cursed Dominion and his evil seed. She cursed her family and their feelings of duty over family, their complete disregard for her well being. She was determined to end it all the first night of mating. Unknown to her maids Trinity had smuggled a silver dagger and a broad sword into the bed chamber. It was suspected an elfin lover supplied her with the weapons, but it was never proven. Finally on the night of mating Dominion again was dragged to mate with Trinity. Again once he got a whiff of her musk his little man took over and the big brain went bye-bye. The minute Dominion mounted Trinity and started thrusting she struck. She grabbed the silver blade from under her pillow and plunged it deep into Dominion's chest. She then took the broad sword and beheaded him. His hard cock was still plunged deep in her cunt. She then grabbed the silver dagger from Dominion's chest and plunged it into her own. They were found an hour later when the healers came to ensure that Dominion had planted his seed. After that, all hell broke loose.

The fathers of both families blamed each other. Other houses and clans refused to embrace this idea of breeding and the whole plan evaporated. No one is certain who struck first. Historians believe that the Crimson Fang brood had tired of peace and wanted revenge, but it could have easily been the Silver Leaf Coven. Long story short, houses and allies took sides and war broke out. The Blood Wars lasted 962 years and killed millions. It decimated every inch of soil on the planet. Whole economies and empires were ruined. By the end there had been so much death and chaos even the most blood thirsty and sanguine of the great houses could no longer stomach the carnage. They wanted peace. They wanted prosperity. But most of all they wanted an assurance that their genetic lines would last and this kind of shit would not happen again."

James took a breath and looked at Rachel to gauge her reaction.

Y"ou with me so far baby?"

"I think so. The whole thing sounds too fantastical...like something out of J.R. Tolkien."

"You would be surprised how much of the Lord of the Rings is actually based on historical accounts and first-hand knowledge. J.R. was a brilliant writer and had a lot of friends from our world help with his writings. Anyway...I need to get back on topic. We need to finish up soon so we can make our party."

"Our party?" she asked intrigued.

"That's right baby. It's our coming out party," James said this with a gay flip of his hand. She rolled her eyes at him, "No serious it's called the Rites of Ascension. You see all werewolf men go through a final transformation the night of their 18th birthday and for the Alpha, it's the time when we first lay claim to our mates. I know what you're thinking...how can a body this gorgeous get any better looking? It's hard but I plan to pull it off. At least I won't be so fucking pale."

Actually, I was thinking that. I think you're already scrumptious right now.

Thanks baby! That means a lot to me. It helps out my male ego and everything. But seriously, I won't look like quite a dork anymore. Although my personality won't change so my inner darkness will still be there. Trust me. You won't be disappointed.

He leaned over and gathered her lips into his own and carefully licked her lower lip. She felt a heat and tingle flow through her. But something was different. She felt the split in her lip fill up and mend and she felt the pain ebb and then it was gone. She looked questioningly at him as if he had pulled a rabbit out of his butt.

"Werewolf saliva has medicinal properties. It also works great as a mild sedative. Relaxes and calms our mates when they are stressed. I've heard a thorough cleaning can be quite sensual and enjoyable. I plan to lick and nibble every edible inch on your delectable body until you scream,"

James said this last part with a lascivious look in his eyes. His emerald green orbs caused her body to flush and all the blood rush to her sex in anticipation of penetration.

"If we don't fuck soon, I am going to scream!" Rachel said with a lustful moan.

"We will babe. Tonight! But I have a few special surprises in store for your birthday. I want to make our first time together special and your first birthday with me unforgettable," James said.

"Is there anything about the clans or the blood war that I should know before we head to the party?" she asked.

"Oh Yeah! Just a little bit more and then we can get going. So in 325 AD Emperor Charlemagne held the first Council of Nicaea in Bithynia, Turkey. A delegation from each race was chosen and sent. It was decided that an everlasting peace was not only wanted but it was dire to the continuation of all the species involved. They decided that there would not be intermingling of blood among the supernatural races. It was discovered that the supernatural races don't mix well together. Much later it was confirmed through genetics. There are too many recessive genes to make mating between an elf and vampire or werewolf and vampire, etc. work. Births would most likely end in death or disfigurement. The genes that make each race unique and give us our powers also disqualifies for interbreeding. Anyway, back to Nicaea. The only race that would guarantee a successful mating was the human race. The human race has no super powers and they share certain traits with all four of the supernatural realms. So the three Fates, you'll meet them tonight, way cool by the way, determined that the Alpha blood lines from each major house would mate with a particular line of humans. Tattoos and identifiable marks for each house and species would be placed on the Alphas and their mates to help identify and find one another. It was up to the clan to protect the mates from harm.

Finally the Fates placed magical and sacred barriers on each mate's sexuality. A female mate would be barren to any other than her mate. This would keep illegitimate births and disputes to bloodlines in power from happening. Secondly, it would help keep mates pure for each other. A male cannot maintain an erection and a female cannot get aroused. Did you ever start to feel queasy or have a stomach ache when you started to kiss or anything with your...ugh...'boyfriends'?" James nearly gagged this last sentence out.

Are you jealous my love?

You have no fucking idea how jealous I was seeing you with that prick Jayden. Each time I saw him touch you I wanted to remove certain parts of his anatomy that would disqualify him from procreating.

That's kind of sweet in a totally possessive, psychopathic kind of way.

James chuckled at this. Rachel's sense of humor drove him round the fucking bend. She was sarcastic, quick witted, and had a sharp of tongue. She was not afraid to get down and nasty in her humor...everything about her made him want to lock her away in his bedroom for days on end and do wholly carnal and unspeakable things to her.

So why don't you?

Huh?! Whoops. Let my imagination run wild again. God, you make me hard!

Rachel reached and grabbed a hold of her man's cock and started to stroke him gently through his jeans.

"You like that baby? You like when I stroke your massive cock for you? You want to take that massive fuck stick and plunge it deep into my tiny fuck hole until I scream and cum all over you, don't you?" Rachel cooed.

"Yesss!" James hissed.

He was quickly losing control. He was so fucking horny he was on the verge of taking her right there. She felt the struggle for control well up in him. She couldn't help but tease him some more. She shifted and bent over the bench presenting her ass to him. The vision alone was driving him mad, not to mention the smell of her arousal sent his wolf through the fucking roof.

"Is this what you want baby? You want to take me like your bitch in heat and make me submit to you like a good submissive bitch don't you big boy? Want to claim my steaming hot cunt for your own, empty your baby batter into my womb, make me fat and pregnant with your babies...is that what you want sweetie?"

Her voice was like gold dipped in honey. But it was the mention of her pregnant with his pups that broke his resolve. He lunged at her knocking her to the ground in a giggling mess of limbs. He straddled her body and forced her arms above her head. He lowered his mouth and nipped at her until she presented her throat to him.

God woman you drive me insane! Do you know what the thought of you pregnant with my pups, your beautiful tits laden with milk does to me? You don't, do you? Well I'll tell you.

He grabbed her hand and shoved it on his crotch. He was hard as steel. His trouser snake was shoved deeply down his pant leg. The denim was causing a painful confinement that was driving him to the point where he didn't care about tonight. He wanted her NOW!

"Oh. Baby! I'm sorry...look what I've done to you. Oh you must be in pain. Let me relieve this for you. Let momma please suck and gobble your fuck stick. Let momma guzzle all that wonderful fuck cream from your massive staff."

James growled low and pulled her to her knees. She practically ripped his jeans down his legs. His cock sprang so quickly it nearly knocked her back. She looked at her new favorite toy with a mischievous glare. She grabbed a hold of him and started stroking him with both hands. His body started to quiver with a sexual tension he had never felt before. Massive amounts of precum started oozing out of his slit. Rachel dove down to retrieve the tasty treat James was offering. She sampled his precum and found it delicious. Something about the taste was just so masculine...a mixture of musk and something that can only be described as James...she needed more. She threw in the towel and dove down his cock like a seasoned whore. She didn't know how she was able to do it, but she managed to down his cock down her throat without gagging. James's eyes rolled back into his head.

Oh my fucking goddess! Luna! How the fuck are you able to do this? You haven't done this before.

I don't know. It tastes so good baby. The smell alone is making me so wet baby. I think I could come just from sucking your cock...oh gods...it tastes so fucking good. Baby I'm having a hard time not mounting you right now. I'm so wet for you. See?

Somewhere between tearing his clothes off and stuffing his hog down her throat Rachel had dexterously unbuttoned and removed her jeans and was now furiously masturbating like a woman possessed while she gobbled his knob like her favorite lollie pop.

Oh fuck! Rachel! Sweetie...I'm too fucking close! If you don't want my cream you better move. I'm going to fucking blow. OH FUCK!

James went off like a fucking roman candle. He had never known an orgasm like the one Rachel was now giving him. He felt like he was dumping a gallon of cum down her throat and she was swallowing like a pro. She acted like it was the sweetest, most delectable essence on this planet. Rachel was swallowing as fast as he was able to spew and he was coming...A LOT! Suddenly Rachel started to twitch and shake as her orgasm took over. Her eyes rolled back into her head as she let go of her release. My God! It felt like she was peeing on him. As perverse as it sounded it excited him more, James managed to find one more shot in the empty barrel of his sperm cannon and deposit it deep into Rachel's throat. Her orgasm had her quaking and shivering like a leaf.

She released his cock from her throat and just continued to shake like she was having a seizure.

"Oh God!" she gasped.

James was suddenly so drained and tired he just needed to lie down.

He lifted her up and gave her a toe tingling kiss to end all kisses. She was moaning and gasping for air. They passed remnants of his cum back and forth. James discovered he didn't mind the taste. They were equal partners in everything. They would share everything...even each other. Finally he released her and she sucked in a lung full of air. She dreamily looked at the man she would spend eternity with and wanted to voice her love but couldn't find the words. So she simply thought.

Did anyone get the number of that bus that hit me? Could you call the driver and have the motherfucker circle around the block?

James broke down laughing. He had tears in his eyes by the end of it. She simply looked at him with the most dreamy, goofy smile on her face and giggled.

"I love you Rachel!"

"I love you James! More than you'll ever know!"

"Oh. I'll know! You're stuck with me whether you like it or not. I can't get you out of my head," he snorted. He had to laugh at his own little joke.

"Dork," she quipped with a yawn.

James quickly shifted into his wolf form and lay down in a patch of soft grass just outside the circle.

Come here baby! Let's take a nap before we head to my house. You're parents and everyone else will be there about six. I think we both need to recharge our batteries so we don't crash tonight. I plan on keeping you up for quite a while tonight. Come snuggle up to me. I'm warm and comfy, just like a furry pillow.

She happily crawled over to her wolf lover...forgetting to even think about modesty and the lack of clothes. She quietly snuggled up to him and closed her eyes. For the first time in her life she felt absolutely at peace. No fears. No worries. Only contentment. She had found her mate...the love of her universe...her life.

I love you James.

I love you baby! So much Rachel! I'm the luckiest immortal on the planet!

Flattery will get you everywhere.

I hope so sweetie...because I plan on being everywhere on your body.

Mmmmm....sounds good baby!

Sweet dreams!

You too!

With that the two lovers slipped happily into unconscious oblivion with dreams of a life filled with love and contentment.

THE END